Christmas Trick or Treat

Christmas Trick or Treat

By Lillie Patterson

Drawings by Kelly Oechsli

GARRARD PUBLISHING COMPANY
CHAMPAIGN, ILLINOIS

To Todd Houston

Library of Congress Cataloging in Publication Data

Patterson, Lillie.
    Christmas trick or treat.

    (First holiday books)
    CONTENTS: Who knocks on Christmas Eve?—Don't forget
the nisse.
    1. Christmas stories. [1. Christmas stories.
2. Short stories] I. Patterson, Lillie. Don't
forget the nisse. 1979. II. Oechsli, Kelly.
III. Title. IV. Series.
PZ7.P2768Ch   [E]   78-11308
ISBN 0-8116-7252-2

Who Knocks on Christmas Eve?

Once there was a poor shoemaker
who had three little boys.
They lived in a mountain village,
high in the Alps.

Most of the people
in the village were poor.
Although the shoemaker worked hard,
he did not make much money.
But he and his sons were cheerful
and had a happy home.
In a corner
of their one-room house
was a long shoemaker's bench.
There the father worked
making and mending shoes.
In another corner
stood a big bed.
Near the fireplace
were a table
and some wooden chairs.
A few pots were by the fireplace.

One winter
the snow was very deep.
The wind blew
through cracks in the house.
The shoemaker and his sons
had only a little cornmeal to eat.
As the December days went by,
the boys were very sad.
"Will we have
a Christmas dinner this year?"
asked Fritz, the youngest.
"I am afraid not,"
said Franz, the middle brother.
"Something good
will happen before Christmas,"
said Friedrich, the oldest.
"You wait and see."

Sure enough, on Christmas Eve
the shoemaker received a letter.
It was from a rich woman
who lived in the valley.
"My best party shoes
must be fixed," she wrote.
"I will need them for Christmas Day.
Please come and mend them."
The shoemaker read the letter
to his sons.
"I must leave you
for the night," he said.
"It will be a long, cold walk
to the woman's house.
But perhaps
I can make enough money
to buy a Christmas dinner."

"We are not afraid to stay alone,"
the boys told him.
"Stay in bed," said their father,
"so you will be warm.
And when I have gone,
lock the door."

The father put on his coat
and long woolen scarf.
He said good-bye to the boys.
Friedrich locked the door
and put a log on the fire.
Then the three boys jumped into bed.

Little Fritz was in the middle.
Franz and Friedrich
were on the sides.
As the hours passed,
they sang songs and told stories.
They talked about the dinner
they might have on Christmas Day.
Suddenly they heard
a loud *knock! knock! knock!*
on the door.
The boys moved close together.
"Maybe it is a hungry wolf,"
Fritz whispered.
Then the noise was louder.
Bang-bang-bang!
"Could it be the wind?"
Franz asked.

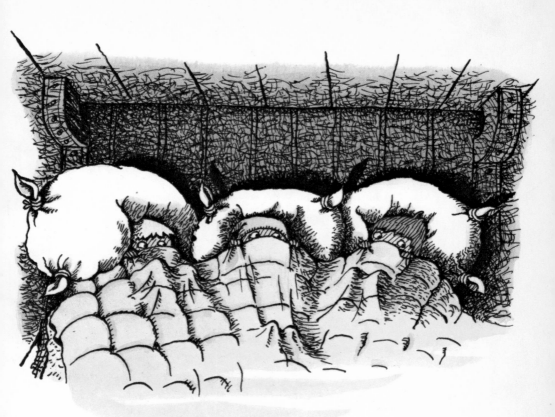

Rat-a-tat-tat!
"Let me come in,"
a voice called.
"Please let me in.
I am cold and very hungry."

"Someone needs help,"
said Friedrich.
He jumped out of the bed.
"Father would want us
to help a poor traveler."
Quickly, he opened the door.
A dwarf came in.
He had a big head,
huge ears, and a round nose.
He was dressed in red.
His long white beard
hung almost to his toes.
"Bad, bad boys,"
said the dwarf.
He seemed angry.
"Why did you leave me
outside in the cold?"

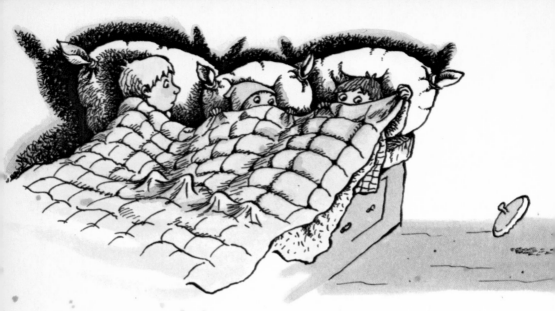

"Our father told us
to keep the door closed,"
the boys said.
"But we thought
you needed help, so we—"
"Bah!" said the little man.
He pushed Friedrich back into bed.
He banged on the pots and pans
and turned them upside down.

"Empty!" he cried.
"Bad, bad boys.
You have eaten
every bit of supper."
"But we have
not eaten all day,"
Franz told the wee man.
"I don't believe you,"
said the visitor.

Now his eyes began to twinkle,
and he hopped into bed
with the boys.
Playfully he pushed them
to one side.
"Give me more of the covers,"
he cried.
The wee man
pinched first one boy,
then another.
He pulled their ears
and tickled their toes.
Frightened, the children lay still.
They did not know what to do.
The dwarf was their guest.
Although he was strange,
they wanted to be nice to him.

At last Friedrich spoke,
"Sir, we are sorry
that we have no food for you.
When our father comes home,
we hope we can give you
a good Christmas dinner."
"Bosh!" said the little man.
He sat up.
"This bed is too crowded,"
he said.
He pointed to Friedrich.
"You are the oldest,
so you get up."
Then the little man
pushed Friedrich
out of the bed.
"Now!" he said.

"Go to the corner
and stand on your head.
Down with your head.
Now, up with your feet!"
Friedrich stood on his head
with his feet in the air.
Bump! Thump! Bumpety-thump!

Christmas goodies started to roll
out of Friedrich's pockets.
Out came nuts of every kind.
Out came apples and oranges
and other good things.
His brothers cried out with joy.
"Ho, ho!" laughed the little man.

He turned to Franz.
"Get out of bed
and let me see
what you can do."
He pushed Franz across the floor.
"Now, let me watch
while you turn cartwheels."
As Franz turned cartwheels,
bright-colored candies
fell out of his pockets.
Pop-pop-kerplop!
There were chocolates, sugar plums,
candy canes, lime drops, gumdrops,
lollipops, mints, and marshmallows.
The boys shouted with joy.
"Now it's your turn,"
the dwarf told Fritz.

He pulled Fritz from the bed.
Franz and Friedrich
helped their little brother
to stand on his head.
Clink! Clink! Clinkety-clank!
Gold and silver coins
fell out of Fritz's pockets.

There were enough
to buy all the food and clothes
they would ever need.
The boys danced about and shouted
as they picked up the good things.
"Thank you," they called,
as they ran toward the bed.

"Thank you for—"
The boys stopped.
The bed was empty,
and the dwarf was gone!
From outside
they heard his merry laugh.
"A merry Christmas to the shoemaker
and to his three fine sons!"
What a tale
the boys told their father
when he came home!
"It must have been
the king of the Little People,"
said the shoemaker with a smile.
"He often comes at Christmas
to play tricks and give surprises
to families who need his help."

The shoemaker and his three sons
had a big Christmas dinner.
As they started to eat,
the boys sang out happily,
"A merry Christmas
to the king of the Little People.
A merry Christmas to everyone."

Don't Forget the Nisse

Once there was a farmer
who had a fine farm.
His crops grew well,
and his cows gave good milk.
The farmer's wife
and all his children were happy.
They worked hard on the farm.

Now on this same farm,
there was a little nisse
who lived in the barn.
The nisse and the farmer
were good friends.
The fairy man watched the crops
and saw that they grew well.
He saw that
the cows gave good milk.
One day
the farmer sold his farm.
"Always be good to the nisse,"
he told the new farmer.
"When Christmas comes,
give him a Christmas pudding.
If you do this,
the nisse will be good to you."

Then the farmer packed his things.
He took his family on a trip
to see the world.
Now the new farmer
did not believe
in fairy folk and magic.
"There is no such thing
as a nisse,"
he said to his wife.
The farmer did not know it,
but the nisse was hiding nearby.
When the nisse heard
what the farmer said,
he became angry.
But then his anger turned to fun.
He decided to play tricks
on that farmer.

The next morning,
the farmer went to the barn
to feed his cows.
While he was getting hay,
the farmer thought he saw
two bright eyes watching him.
"That must be the cat,"
the farmer thought.

"Get out of here, cat,"
he shouted.
The farmer picked up a stick
and started to chase the cat.
Suddenly he fell over the stick
and sat down hard on the floor.
Then he thought he saw
a little man wearing a red cap.

The little man
was laughing so hard
his red cap almost fell off.
"Fiddle-faddle!"
the farmer cried.
"That fall made me think
I saw a little man."
As the days went by
the farmer worked hard.
Now the crops were in the barn,
and the leaves changed color.
Soon winter came.
The farmer and his family
were getting ready for Christmas.
The nisse watched all they did.
He smiled when the farmer's wife
made the Christmas puddings.

"Christmas pudding,
good Christmas pudding,"
he sang to himself.
"It is almost time
for my Christmas pudding."

At last it was Christmas Eve.

The nisse went to the barn.

He looked everywhere

for his Christmas pudding.

He looked and he looked.

He rubbed his eyes

and looked some more.

But there was no Christmas pudding

for the tiny nisse.

The new farmer

had not left any for him!

The nisse ran back to the house.

He peeped through the window.

The farmer's family

was eating a big dinner.

And there, on the table,

was a golden Christmas pudding!

The wee nisse was very hungry.
He wiped a tear from his eye.
Nobody had thought about him.
He was sad as he went back
to the barn.
He did not have
a happy Christmas that year.
After the Christmas holidays,
strange things happened on the farm.
One night the farmer's wife
heard a loud crash in the kitchen.
It sounded as if the dishes
were being thrown around.
"Oh, my!" cried the farmer's wife.
She ran into the kitchen.
There she found
all of the dishes on the floor.

But not one had been broken!
"How can this be?
Who did this?" she cried.
The nisse watched
from his hiding place.
How he laughed!

Then, quick as a flash,

the nisse jumped out the window.

The next day,

the farmer went to the barn.

Suddenly

something hit him from behind.

He looked around,

but no one was there.

Then something hit him

on his neck.

He was hit on his head,

his arms, and his legs.

The farmer was hit so fast,

he could not get away.

While he hopped about in pain,

he thought he saw a tiny man

with a stick in each hand.

The tiny man
went on hitting the farmer.
And he sang a merry song:
   Now, do you believe in nisses?
   Now, do you believe in nisses?
   Now, do you believe in nisses?
   You poor, poor farmer!
Slowly the farmer
went back to his house.
He went right to bed.
"Did I really see
a tiny man in the barn?"
he thought to himself.
"Could it have been a nisse?"
After a few days,
the farmer felt better.
"I must have had a dream," he said.

"I must have dreamed
that I saw a nisse.
I still do not believe
there is a nisse."
The farmer went back to work.
But everything seemed to go wrong.
The crops were poor.
The cows gave very thin milk.
Finally he went to see the man
who had sold him the farm.
"Please tell me what to do,"
he asked the other farmer.
"Are you taking
good care of the nisse?"
the first farmer asked.
"Did you give him
a Christmas pudding?"

"No," said the new farmer.

"The nisse is angry with you,"
the first farmer said.

"Things will not go right
until you give him
a golden pudding at Christmas."

The sad farmer went home.

"Maybe—," he told his wife,

"maybe there is a nisse after all."

"I'll make a pudding

for the nisse this Christmas,"

the farmer's wife said.

Christmas Eve came once more.

The farmer's wife

made the Christmas puddings.

She made a special one

for the nisse.

The farmer came into the kitchen.

"Is this the pudding

for the nisse?" he asked.

"Did you put in rich cream

and many cups of raisins?"

"Yes," said the farmer's wife.

Carefully, the farmer took
the golden Christmas pudding
to the barn.
He put it down
on a clean white cloth.
"This is for our nisse," he whispered.
He looked about for the little man.
But the farmer did not see him.

The next morning
the pudding was gone.
And under the Christmas tree,
there were lots of presents
for the farmer's children.

Everyone on the farm
had a fine Christmas.
From that day on
the nisse and the farmer
were good friends.

The crops grew well,
and the cows gave rich milk.
The farmer never again
forgot to give the nisse
a golden Christmas pudding.